A GIFT-BEAR FOR THE KING

ILLUSTRATED BY LILLIAN HOBAN

WEEKLY READER CHILDREN'S BOOK CLUB

presents

A Gift-Bear
FOR THE King

BY CARL MEMLING

E. P. DUTTON & CO., INC.　NEW YORK

For Pearl

There was once an old man and an old woman who lived in a hut in a forest. They were very poor, but they had a little bear cub for a friend.

This bear cub could stand on his front paws.

5

He could add and spell.

He could wash dishes.

And what a lovely
singing voice he had!
   The old man and the old
woman loved to hear him sing
himself to sleep at night.
And so did all the forest
birds.

One day a man rode by the hut. He called out, "Our King is having a birthday! Our King is having a birthday!"

The old man and the old woman were very fond of their King. So they went inside and got busy looking for a birthday gift.

They looked all around the hut, but found nothing.
"Oh," they said sadly, "if we only had something
fine enough to send the King."

"But you have," said the bear cub. "Why not send me?"
Their little bear cub a gift–bear for the King?
At first they refused.

"Why not?" said the bear cub. "Send me. What
must be, must be."

The old man sighed and got a gift card.

The old woman tied the card around the bear cub's neck.

How pretty he looked!

"Go now, Gift-Bear," they said sadly. "You must get to the King on time for his birthday."

"I will," said Gift-Bear.

"Don't get lost," they said.

"I won't," said Gift-Bear.

Down the road he went. And as he went, he sang
this song:

> *I'm the gift-bear*
> *for the King—*
> *I won't stop*
> *for anything.*

The road he followed went past fields and farms
and over hills and streams.

He had not gone too far, when he saw a circus tent
with a sign on it that said, "CLOSED."

Gift-Bear stopped.

"I wonder why it's closed," he said. "I'll find out, and then be on my way."

He looked around, and at last he found the circus owner.

"Hello there," he said. "Is anything wrong?"

The owner nodded. "I had to close my circus because I have no acrobat. Somehow I'll have to get an acrobat," he said.

"Let me see," said Gift-Bear. "I can stand on my front paws."

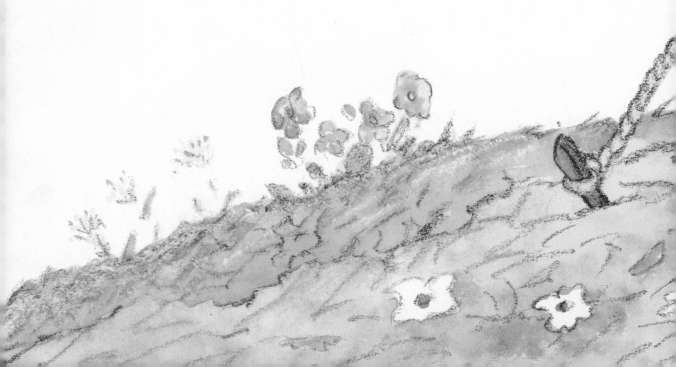

What a fine idea—a gift-bear as an acrobat!

At once the circus owner took down the "CLOSED" sign and put another sign up.

In big, bold, blazing letters the new sign said:

THE ONE AND ONLY
WORLD FAMOUS
GIFT-BEAR
COME ONE · COME ALL
TO SEE
HIS ACROBATIC TRICKS
TODAY

A big crowd came to the circus.

There was a loud, long roll of drums.

And then Gift–Bear went all the way across the high wire on his front paws.

Next he did some fancy flip-flops.

Then he flew on the flying trapeze.

And everybody clapped and cheered
for the daring bear cub.

Days passed, and weeks passed.

Everywhere the circus went, Gift-Bear went along until at last . . .

. . . another acrobat came.

"Goodby," called Gift-Bear to all his circus friends.

Down the road he went again.
And as he went, he sang his song:

> I'm the gift-bear
>   for the King—
> I won't stop
>   for anything.

It was not long before he came to
a little schoolhouse. In front of the school,
by the side of the road, seven gloomy children sat.

Gift–Bear stopped.

This won't take long, he thought. I have a way
with children.

In his most cheerful voice he called, "Hello there.
Why so gloomy?"

"That's why," said the children, pointing behind them. "We have a school, but we have no teacher. Without a teacher, what good is a school?"

"Now let me see," said Gift-Bear. "What must be, must be. But *this* must not be. I can add. I can spell. And *someone* must teach these children."

What a fine teacher
Gift–Bear was!
He wore eyeglasses.
And he wrote on the
blackboard with chalk.

Gift–Bear taught the
children 1 plus 1.
He taught them A, B, C.

He even taught them how to stand on their hands.

Gift–Bear taught
and taught
and taught the children,
until, at last . . .

. . . another teacher came.

"Goodby," said Gift-Bear, springing up. "I must
be on my way."

And down the road he went again, as fast as he could,
singing his song:

> *I'm the gift-bear*
> > *for the King—*
> *I won't stop*
> > *for anything.*

Soon he came to an inn.

"I can't stop here," said Gift-Bear. "I must get
to the King on time."

Just then the innkeeper came running out.

"Stop!" he called. "Stop, stop, STOP!"

Gift-Bear sighed and stopped.

"Anything wrong?" he asked.

"Come," said the innkeeper. "See for yourself."

They went inside. And the innkeeper pointed to
at least a thousand dishes in a great pile on the floor.

"If I can't get those dishes washed," he said,
"I'll have to close the inn. Would you, by any chance,
know of a good dishwasher?"

"I would," said Gift-Bear sadly. "I can wash dishes."

Gift–Bear started washing.
He washed dishes . . .

and dishes . . .
and dishes . . .
and dishes.

Oh, how glad Gift-Bear was when
at last they were finished!
"Goodby!" he called.

He ran down the road until he came to the
King's palace.

"Well, hello," said Gift-Bear to the guards at the
gate. "Happy birthday to the King."

All the guards glared at the gift card.

They said, "The King's birthday was months ago.
Why didn't you get to him on time?"

"I stopped for a few things," said Gift-Bear.

"THAT'S NO EXCUSE FOR BEING LATE!" roared
the guards.

"LOCK HIM UP IN THE DUNGEON!"
bellowed the Captain of the Guard.

And into the dungeon they shoved poor Gift–Bear.
"Clang!" went the dungeon door.
Gift–Bear was all alone.

"Don't be sad," he told himself.
But he was very sad.
And he sang a sad song:

> *I was the gift–bear*
> *   for the King—*
> *But I stopped*
> *   for everything.*
> *Once I was glad*
> *   but now I am sad—*
> *Locked up here*
> *   in the King's dungeon.*

"My, what a lovely singing voice that is!" said
some bluebirds on the palace wall. "And what a sad
and lovely song!"

Off flew the bluebirds. And as they flew,
they sang the bear cub's sad song.

Poor Gift–Bear.

Many days went by.
Many,
        many
            days . . .

At last, one day, the dungeon door opened. The Captain
of the Guard came in. And then the King himself came in.
Next the innkeeper came in. Then the schoolchildren.
And then all of Gift-Bear's circus friends.

"Gift–Bear," his friends told him, "we heard the bluebirds sing your song. So we came to tell the King why you were late."

"Good little helpful Gift–Bear!" said the King. "I didn't even know you were here."

"I want to thank the old man and the old woman for sending you," said the King.

"Can you take me to them?"
the King asked Gift-Bear.

"I can," said Gift-Bear.

"Do you know the way?" said the King.

"I do," said Gift-Bear.

They all went down the road
until they came to the hut in the forest.

Gift-Bear and the King went in.

The King said to the old man and the old woman,

"A thousand thanks for the finest gift ever sent a King."

"I want you to live in the palace with Gift-Bear
and me," the King said. "Will you come?"

"They will," said Gift-Bear. "What must be, must be."

So down the road they all went again.
And as they went, Gift-Bear danced and sang:

I'm the gift-bear
for the King—
I didn't stop
for anything.
Well,
hardly
anything . . .